Dedicated to Tommy George and Don Hemby,

my two buddies from high school

who instilled the possibility of adventure in my heart.

And for Kevin Bennett who has been my friend since second grade.

The time has flown...

Chic

Dedicated to my siblings-

Marganne, Bill, Clay, Cecelia, Liza, Kyle, Virginia Lee, and Harlan.

I am truly blessed and love you all!

Thelma Kat

COOLWATERRIPPLE
GROUP®

With special thanks to the Cool Water Ripple Group® Family
www.CoolWaterRippleGroup.com

Credits:
Written by: Chic Cariaga and the Students of Strong Foundations Homeschool Co-op
Illustrated by: Thelma Kathleen Ferry
Designed by: Kim Trimble Hall
Creative editor: Kathy Lewis
Edited by: Jennifer Brown McElhaney and Pam Tuggle Wetherington

Library of Congress CIP applied for.
ISBN # 978-1-7323236-1-2

NO ONE
GOES EVERYWHERE

Story by Chic Cariaga   Illustrations by Thelma Kat Ferry

I have a dog.
I named him No One.

1

He loves to travel, and
No One goes everywhere.

Ireland is one of No One's favorite places. He goes to kiss the Blarney Stone.

No One goes to London to see
Big Ben! He takes Some One to go
see a Shakespearean play.

No One goes to Paris to see the Eiffel Tower. He wants to see the Mona Lisa in the Louvre Museum. No One likes to eat macaroons and baguettes by the river Seine.

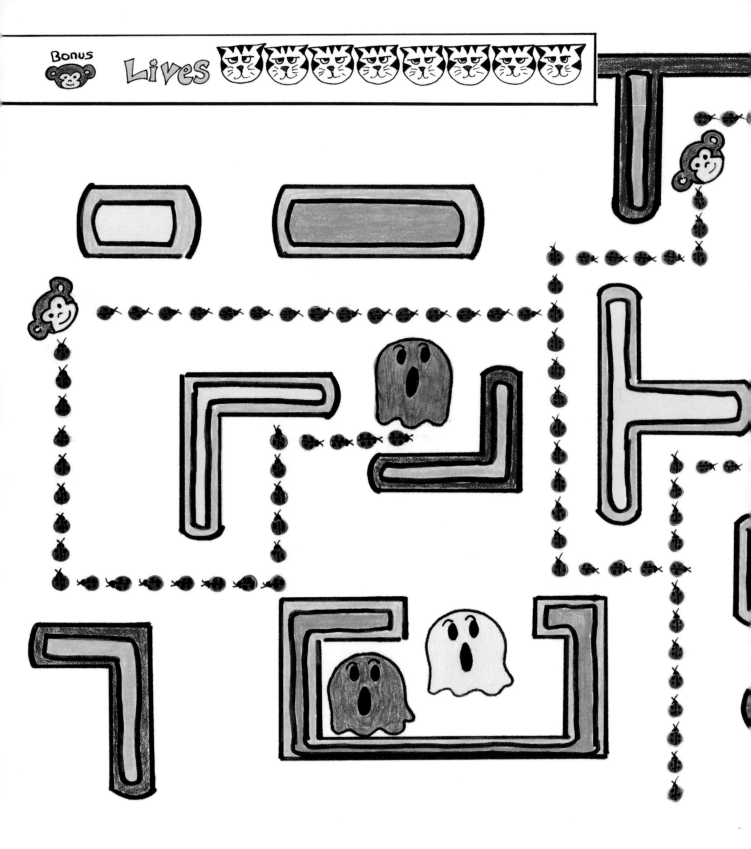

No One wants to play in
Video Game World.

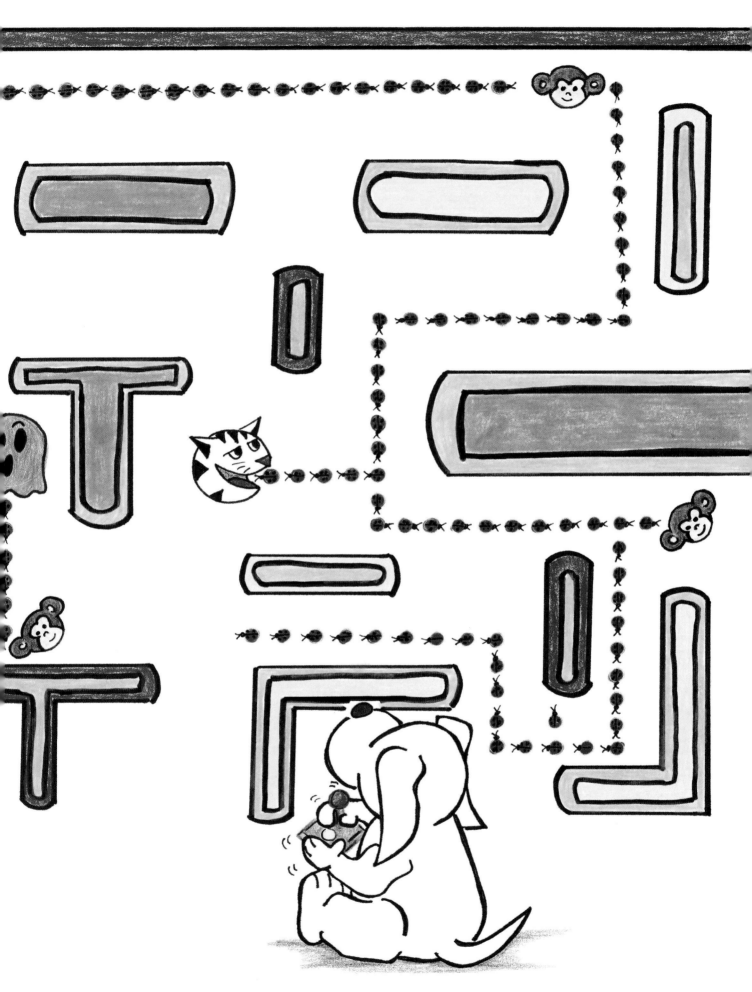

No One believes he was once a Pharaoh's Royal Dog in Ancient Egypt. No One rushes to Giza to buy pottery.

Playing in the hot sand of the Sahara Desert is one of No One's favorite activities.

No One goes to the Philippines and searches for the beautiful Philippine Eagle!

No One goes to a restaurant that has sushi in Tokyo's Tsukiji Fish Market. No One also goes to the Kabuki-za Theater.

No One loves to go to the Moon to experience the craters! He wants to see an alien to learn how to speak alien. No One learned how to fly a UFO.

Hanging loose in Hawaii, No One goes to Honolulu and surfs at Waikiki Beach.

No One likes tostados,
so No One goes to Mexico.

No One likes to swim in a swimming pool.
Some One likes to eat yummy fish food!

Rock climbing at Scout Camp is something No One happily anticipates. No One also wants to go on a hot air balloon ride and eat smores.

Hiking to Tahquamenon Falls, *No One* goes sailing and catches a fish on Lake Michigan.

No One loves big boats and wants to ride big, scary waterslides on a cruise ship!

No One wants to go to Chincoteague Island and see the majestic horses!

After visiting Maine's Casco Bay,
No One goes to ski on
Mount Katahdin.

No One wants to walk across the Brooklyn Bridge. He and Some One stay in a fancy hotel with yummy room service.

No One ends his world trip in Florida. He plays on a beach, takes a long, peaceful nap under a palm tree and dreams…

Some One was exhausted from the world travels; but No One was busy preparing for the next adventure…

No One likes
his friend's artwork

1.

2.

3.

4.

5.

6.

7.

8.

9.

10.

11.

12.

13.

14.

15.

16.

17.

18.

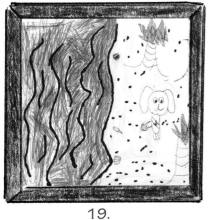

19.

Some One thinks they are great too!

Strong Foundations Students

Strong Foundations is a homeschool co-op located in Union County
North Carolina. It was founded in 2015. We offer elective style classes for
Pre-K through 5th grade. We offer families fun learning opportunities as well
as growth in friendship and support in homeschooling.

Strong Foundations Bios/Artwork Credits

1. Olivia Groening 7, 2nd grade – Loves arts and crafts and wants to be an artist, chef, and baker when she grows up.

2. Bella Ryals 7, 2nd grade – Loves animals, horseback riding, ballet, and reading and wants to do something with animals when she grows up.

3. Meredith McElhaney 8, 3rd grade – Loves to cook and wants to be a missionary when she grows up.

4. Joshua McBride 9, 3rd grade – Wants to produce online viral videos when he grows up.

5. Hunter Shipley 9, 3rd grade – Wants to be a video game programmer when he grows up.

6. Noah Holman 6, 1st grade – Wants to be a paramedic when he grows up.

7. Corabelle Groening 6, Kindergarten – Loves to draw and color and wants to be an artist and a nurse when she grows up.

8. Kaia Langille 7, 2nd grade – Wants to be a famous singer when she grows up. Likes to dance.

9. Ricky Phillips 9, 3rd grade – Love to build with Legos and wood and wants to be a writer when he grows up.

10. Riley Langille 10, 4th grade – Wants to be the President of the United States when she grows up. She likes to do art projects.

11. Joseph Briney 5, Kindergarten – Loves playing cards with mommy and wants to be a firefighter when he grows up.

12. Some One 7, 2nd Grade – Loves eating cupcakes and hiding from No One. He wants to be a tiger when he grows up.

13. Jeremiah Briney 8, 2nd grade – Loves to read, build forts with his family, go to co-op, and wants to be a firefighter when he grows up.

14. James Briney 7, 1st grade – Loves playing Legos and building things out of wood with daddy and wants to be a daddy when he grows up.

15. Lily McElhaney 6, 1st grade – Loves dogs and wants to be a super hero when she grows up.

16. Emily Grant 5, Kindergarten – Wants to be a veterinarian and a mommy when she grows up.

17. Grace Comstock 7, 2nd grade – Wants to be a gymnast and a veterinarian when she grows up.

18. Matthew McBride 6, 1st grade – Loves animals and wants to be an animal trainer when he grows up.

19. Amanda Shirlen 8, 3rd grade – Loves cats and wants to be a veterinarian when she grows up.

Chic Cariaga is a writer with wanderlust in his heart. He has traveled extensively in North American having visited all but a handful of the United States and Canadian provinces, plus Mexico. The Caribbean is a favorite destination as is Europe. The US National Park system is also a favorite and he encourages everyone to go and visit "America's Best Idea" as much as possible.

Thelma Kat Ferry grew up in the small town of LaGrange, Georgia and the youngest of nine children. At an early age, she discovered the love of drawing using crayons and paper. Throughout grade school and into high school, she could always be found in the art room creating illustrations and honing in on her craft. Encouraged to pursue her love for art, she attended LaGrange College where she received her Bachelors Degree in Art and Design. Whether it's crayons, colored pencils, acrylics, or watercolor paints, she can always be found in her studio bringing stories to life with her illustrations. Thelma Kat lives in New Jersey with her husband and two sons.

You are welcomed to come visit our website anytime and view our current book offerings. Request or search for our published books at your favorite retailer...

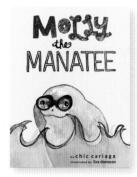

"Molly the Manatee"

© 2016 Author Chic Cariaga

Illustrated by Liza Donovan

"A Grandiose Gathering"

© 2017 Author Chic Cariaga

Illustrated by Thelma Kat Ferry

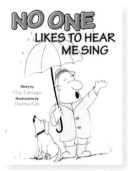

"No One Likes to Hear Me Sing"

© 2017 Author Chic Cariaga

Illustrated by Thelma Kat Ferry

"Bosco"

© 2017 Author Chic Cariaga

Illustrated by Thelma Kat Ferry

"Cucumber Flamingo"

© 2018 Author Chic Cariaga &

Katelyn Hartwick

Illustrated by Thelma Kat Ferry

"No One Likes Second Grade"

© 2017 Author Chic Cariaga

Illustrated by Thelma Kat Ferry

"Introducing Miss Behaving"

© 2018 Author Lisa Rupp

Illustrated by Thelma Kat Ferry

Please shop: www.coolwaterripplegroup.com